My Own Grandpa

By Leone Castell Anderson
Illustrated by Kathy Wilburn

A Golden Book • New York
Western Publishing Company, Inc., Racine, Wisconsin 53404

D1371992

Andrew dragged his feet. He sighed. He looked at his ball.
It was no fun playing when there was no one to play with.
All of his friends were away on vacation.

Suddenly Andrew remembered that his friend Ben was still home. He ran down the block. "Ben," he yelled. "Want to play catch?"

"Hi, Andrew. Can't. Grandpa and me are going to play checkers."

"Oh." Andrew slowed. "How about when you're through with checkers?"

"Can't." Ben shook his head. "Grandpa's going to take me fishing."

Andrew trudged home. He wished he had a grandpa
who lived nearby. A grandpa to go fishing with. A grandpa
to do things with.

Andrew tossed his ball up in the air. It came down and
bounced once, then twice. Then, bump, bump, bump, it
bounced toward the street. Andrew started for the curb.

"Don't go out in that street, young man!" It was a billy-goat-gruff voice.

Andrew turned around. A man with bushy white eyebrows was glaring at him. The man looked scary to Andrew.

"I wasn't going in the street," Andrew said.

"Hmph. Good thing," said the man.

Andrew stomped over to the curb. He picked up the ball from where it had rolled into the gutter. Then he stomped home.

"Boy!" he said. "A grumpy old man yelled at me, and Ben's busy with his grandpa, and there's nobody to play with. I wish *I* had a grandpa to do things with."

"You sound as if you're lonesome." His mother hugged him to her. "Andrew," she said, "I think it's time you met the people I work with. They're sometimes lonesome, too."

"You mean the people who live in that big green house around the corner?" Andrew knew the green house was called Green Meadows Manor. His mother went to work there once a week. But Andrew had never gone there with her.

His mother smiled and took his hand. "That's right," she said. "Let's go."

Inside the house, in a large sunny room, lots of people were busy. Many of them smiled and said hello.

A gray-haired lady looked up from her knitting. "Are you going to give us a painting lesson today?" she asked Andrew's mother.

"Not today, Mrs. Bailey. Today I brought my son, Andrew, to meet all my friends here."

Andrew's mother took him around the room. Andrew liked the man with no hair and thick glasses. When Andrew couldn't say "Giannopoulos," the man smiled and said to call him Mr. G.

Mrs. Wilson showed Andrew how she made her wheelchair go.

When his mother stopped to chat with Mrs. Wilson, Andrew skipped on ahead. He wanted to meet everyone.

He saw a man sitting at a table. Andrew went over to him. "Hi," he said.

The man squinted up at him. "You're in my light, young
man," he said.

Andrew stiffened. It was the man with the bushy
eyebrows and gruff voice.

"I'm not a young man," Andrew said. "I'm Andrew."
He didn't like this man. He turned away.

"So you're Andrew." The man's voice didn't sound
nearly so gruff this time. Andrew slowly turned back.

"Well, I'm William. William Barker," said the man. He held out his hand.

He wasn't smiling, Andrew saw. But his eyes looked twinkly under those bushy eyebrows. He wasn't quite so scary now.

Andrew shook the man's hand. "Hi," he said.

"I'm tying flies," Mr. Barker told him.

"Tying flies?" asked Andrew.

"Flies," Mr. Barker said. "To fish with. Haven't you ever gone fishing?"

"Yes, I have," Andrew said. "My daddy took me. We fished off a bridge. But we didn't have flies."

William Barker chuckled.

"He isn't scary at all when he laughs," Andrew thought.

"Fly-fishing is something special, Andrew. Look here."
He showed Andrew a box. It was filled with bright-colored
bits of feathers.

"Those are flies," said Mr. Barker. "You tie one of those
on the end of a line. Cast. Reel in. Keep that fly skimming
along the water..."

Mr. Barker was pretending with an imaginary rod and reel. Andrew watched him.

"Then, suddenly," said Mr. Barker, "*wham*! That old trout takes the fly and..."

Andrew giggled at Mr. Barker reeling in a fish they couldn't even see. But it looked like fun.

"Do you think I could do that?" Andrew asked.

Mr. Barker looked at him. "Would you like me to take you fly-fishing?"

"Boy! Sure," Andrew cried. He grinned at Mr. Barker.

Suddenly Andrew asked, "Would you be my grandpa?" Then he frowned. "But I guess you already belong to somebody else."

"I do have three grandchildren, Andrew," said Mr. Barker. "But they all live far away."

"My grandpa lives far away, too," said Andrew.

"Then it's a deal," said Mr. Barker. They shook hands again.

Just then Andrew's mother came up. "Hello, Mr. Barker," she said. "I see that you and Andrew have met."

"Mrs. Mitchell," Mr. Barker said, "may I take your son fishing tomorrow?"

She looked at the two of them and smiled. "I think that's a great idea," she said.

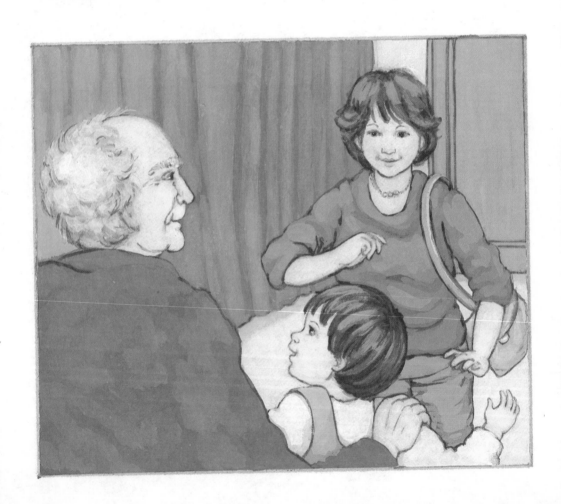

"Good," said Mr. Barker. "I'll come by about eight in the morning. Better be ready, Andrew."

"Yes, sir." Andrew turned and waved at Mr. Barker as he and his mother went toward the door.

Andrew skipped on the way home. As they were passing Ben's house Ben came out the door. "Hey, Andrew," he called. "Want to go fishing tomorrow with my grandpa and me?"

Andrew smiled. "Can't," he said. "I'm going fishing with my own grandpa."